Raging Rapids

by PATTY BRISCO

CREATIVE EDUCATION, INC.

Illustrated by Kevin Davidson

Managing Editor: Dolly Hasinbiller
Project Editor: Lisa Eisenberg

Published by Creative Education, Inc., 123 South Broad Street, Mankato, Minnesota 56001. Copyright © 1978 Bowmar/Noble, Publishers, Inc. All rights reserved subject to the provisions of the copyright revision act of 1976 [PL. 94-553 (S. 22)]. Printed in the United States.

Library of Congress cataloging in publication data:

Brisco, Patty
Raging Rapids

78-71859   ISBN 0-87191-683-5

Contents

Chapter 1

Lost in the Woods

Mike Trent climbed down from the bus. He put his bag down on the ground. Then the bus drove away in a cloud of dust. Mike was left alone by the side of the road.

Where was his Grandfather Hinshaw? The old man was supposed to meet him here. Mike looked around. But he couldn't see anyone or anything. There were only the tall trees and the empty road.

All at once, Mike heard a loud growl. It came from behind him. He turned. A big, brown dog was running toward him. It had a wide, red mouth and long, yellow teeth. A yell caught in Mike's throat.

The big animal was about to jump on him. Then a voice cried out, "Stop it, Canardly! You stop it right now!"

The animal dropped down on all fours. It sat looking at Mike. Mike took a deep breath and looked back. He was shaking.

Behind the dog stood a man. He was thin and tough-looking. He had a brown face and short white hair.

Mike guessed that the man was his grandfather. Mike knew only one thing about him. The old man had not talked to Mike's mother for many years. It had something to do with her leaving home and marrying Mike's father.

But Mike's father had died several years ago. Now his mother was very sick. She would have to stay in the hospital for a long time. They had no other family, so Mike had been sent to stay with his grandfather.

Finally, the old man spoke. "Well," he said. "You're Elsie's kid. I can tell by the eyes and the mouth. You have the Hinshaw eyes and mouth."

"Hello, Grandfather," said Mike.

The old man shook his head. "Don't go calling me *that*, young man. You can call me Hank. Everybody else does."

Mike swallowed. He had had no way of knowing what his grandfather would be like. But still, he had not been prepared for this.

"All right, Hank," he said.

"And this is Canardly." Hank pointed to the dog. "He is not as mean as he acts. But don't you ever tell him that."

Mike looked at the dog. "Canardly?" Mike said. "That seems like kind of a funny name. Why do you call him that?"

For the first time, Hank almost smiled. "Because you 'can hardly' tell what kind of dog he is," he said.

Mike laughed. "That's really funny!" he said. He smiled at his grandfather.

But Hank's face was serious again. "Come along now," he said. "We have a long walk to the cabin."

Hank turned back the way he had come. Mike could see a winding dirt path. It went off into the woods. The trees grew close together. The thick branches blocked out the sun.

"Do you live back in there?" Mike asked.

Hank nodded. "Of course," he said. "The Hinshaws have always lived in the woods. Except for your mother."

Hank and Canardly started down the path. There was nothing for Mike to do but follow.

His bag was heavy. It kept banging against his knees. But Hank did not offer to help him with it. He walked on into the woods without saying a word. In a few minutes, Mike was far behind. The path went in and out through the forest. Mike soon lost sight of Hank and Canardly.

There were all kinds of sounds in the trees and bushes. Mike heard a lot of strange cries. He supposed they were made by birds. At least, he *hoped* they were made by birds. All of a sudden, he longed for the sounds of cars, the noise of horns, and the voices of people. He wished he were back in the city.

He was beginning to feel very sorry for himself. In fact, he felt so bad that he didn't notice where he was going. He didn't know that he had walked the wrong way.

Then, all at once, he looked around. He saw nothing but trees and bushes. The winding dirt path was gone.

Chapter 2

Hank's Cabin

Oh no! thought Mike. I'm lost.

The wind was blowing hard. Mike felt the cold through his thin jacket. Where in the world were Hank and Canardly?

He put his suitcase down. He sat on the end of it. He could think of only one thing to do—call Hank. So Mike called out as loudly as he could, "Hank! Canardly!"

He opened his mouth to call again. Then Canardly came through the bushes and ran up to him. In a few seconds, Hank followed.

"Quiet, boy!" Hank said crossly. "No need to start yelling."

Mike felt his face getting hot. "I just thought it would make it easier for you to find me," he said. His voice came out louder than he meant it to.

Hank shook his head. "Boy, I have tracked wolf and bear and much stranger things through these woods. It's no problem to track one lost city boy! Besides, you are only a few feet from the path! I would have missed you sooner. But I didn't know you were so far behind."

"I have always been told," said Mike, "that it's best to stay in one place if you are lost. So that's what I did!"

Hank looked at him. For a moment Mike thought he saw a quick smile cross the old man's face.

"Well, I guess staying put is better than running wild through the woods," Hank said. "But in this case, it might have been better if you had moved a bit."

Mike wondered what Hank meant. But before he could ask, Hank picked up the suitcase and headed into the brush.

"Come along now," Hank said. "We still have a ways to go."

At last, they came through the brush. They were standing in the middle of a large open space in the woods.

It was almost dark. But Mike could see the building in front of them.

Hank pointed to it. "Well, there it is, boy. That's the Hinshaw cabin. It's been there for 70 years. It was built by my father—your great-grandfather, Ezra.

Hank said these words proudly. It was clear to Mike that his grandfather loved the cabin. But Mike saw it through different eyes. To him, it didn't look like a real house. It was like something from the Old West.

Hank walked up to the cabin. He opened the door. Mike followed him inside. There was something running around on the floor! Mike jumped back. Canardly started to bark loudly.

"Only a pack rat," said Hank. He laughed out loud. Then he lit a lamp.

Mike found himself growing angry. Hank seemed to be laughing at everything he did. Mike didn't think it was funny at all.

He could see that the lamp Hank had lit was very old. It had a bell-shaped glass top. There was a small fire burning inside it. No electricity. That meant no TV.

"You can sleep over there," said Hank. He pointed to one corner of the room. There was a low bed made of wood. Some furs were piled on top of the bed. Mike didn't think it looked very comfortable.

"Now," said Hank. "I'll get some hot water. You can take a bath. Then we will have supper."

"A bath!" said Mike. "I just had one before I got on the bus."

"You need another one. Take my word for it." Hank was almost smiling. "You were so proud of staying in one place when you were lost. I didn't want to tell you then. But you were right in the middle of some poison oak!"

"Poison oak!" Mike said. "Oh no!" One of his friends had walked in poison oak on a camping trip. Mike knew that his friend had felt bad for several days.

"I can't believe all this is happening to me!" he said to himself.

His grandfather got out a big tub. Mike began to wonder how long he would be able to take this kind of life. Then he began to itch all over his body.

Hank was starting a fire in a big, black stove. Then he put a pot of water on to heat.

This sure is some place Mom sent me to, Mike thought.

Mike took a bath in the tub. Hank made them something to eat. Then they went to bed.

Mike was almost asleep when the howling started. It was a wild, strange sound. Mike felt cold under his fur bed covering. He wished he were back in the city. In the city, he knew what the noises were.

14

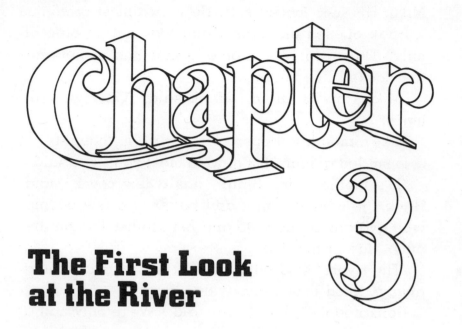

Chapter 3

The First Look at the River

Hank woke Mike up early the next morning. The sun was just coming up over the trees.

Mike had not slept well. He had scratched himself all night. And the howling had kept him awake.

Hank gave him something for the poison oak. Mike felt better in a few minutes. He started to put on his shoes. Then he heard a knock at the door.

Hank went to the door. He opened it wide. A boy about Mike's age stood outside. He had a basket on his arm. He held the basket out to Hank.

Hank took it. "Come in," he said to the boy.

The boy came into the cabin. He was smaller than Mike. His face looked soft. He was almost pretty.

Hank opened the basket and took out a bottle of milk. There was also some cream and something that looked like butter.

"Mike, this is Joline," Hank said. "Only we call her Jo."

Mike's mouth fell open. It's a girl! he thought.

Jo smiled at him. "I'm glad to meet you," she said.

"Jo's mother, Mrs. Smith, has a few cows," said Hank. "Jo sells the milk and butter to a few people who live around here. Jo and her mother live on the other side of the river."

"The river?" said Mike. He felt interested. He had always liked lakes and rivers.

Hank nodded. "Right," he said. "We're only half a mile from the river. There's good fishing. And you can even swim under the bridge. But it gets a bit rough farther down. That's at the rapids."

"Oh!" said Mike. "I would really like to see it."

Hank shrugged. "Why don't you go with Jo?" he said. "You can help her finish her deliveries. She can show you the river. It will help you get to know the country. Here!"

He threw Mike some cheese, a thick piece of bread, and an apple. "You can eat breakfast along the way," he said.

Mike was not sure that he wanted to go with this strange girl. But he did want to see the river. "All right," he said to Hank.

At first he didn't know what to say to Jo. She didn't seem to have much to say, either. But pretty soon

Mike felt that he had to say *something*. "How long have you lived around here?" he asked.

"All my life," said Jo.

"How do you stand it?" Mike said. "I mean, what do you *do*? There's nothing around here but trees and animals. My grandfather doesn't even have electricity! There's no TV. Not even radio. There are no movies. There's not even a place to buy comic books! It's just like an old movie!"

Jo turned. She looked at him. Her face was kind of pink. Mike thought she looked angry.

Jo shook her head. "That shows what you know," she said. "The people up here *do* have electricity—if they want it. Your grandfather just likes to live the old way. You know something? I feel sorry for you! All you can think about are comic books and TV. Why, there's so much to do here, I never have time to do all the things I want. I fish. I walk in the woods. I swim in the river. But I guess you don't know about those kinds of things. You are just a city boy!"

The way she said "city boy" made the words sound like a bad name. But Jo kept on. "You are just a tenderfoot! If I left you alone out here, you would be lost in five minutes!"

Mike felt silly. He would have liked to say something back. But he knew she was right. He knew he should not have said all those things about life out here. This was Jo's home.

"I'm sorry," he said. "I should never have said what I did. Let's start over again, all right?"

Jo thought about it for a moment. Then she smiled back. "All right," she said.

Just then, they came out of the woods. In front of
them was the river. It was beautiful. Mike's eyes
grew wide as he looked at it. There's nothing like
this in the city, he thought. He knew now what he
wanted most in the world. It was to ride a boat
down this river.

Chapter 4

Finding the Boat

Mike turned to Jo. "Wow!" he said. "I never saw a river this big before."

Jo smiled. Mike walked over to the river's edge. He looked down. The water seemed to be moving very fast. "Have you ever gone down the river in a boat?" he asked Jo.

Jo shook her head. "No," she said. "But my Uncle Bob has. He is a guide. In the summer, he takes people down the rapids. But it's dangerous. My mother won't let me go until I'm a lot older."

Mike looked down the river. "I don't see any rapids," he said.

Jo pointed. "They are down the river a few miles," she said. "Almost every year somebody loses a boat or two, trying to ride them. Two years ago, a man was killed!"

"Wow!" Mike said again. He was thinking of a movie he had seen. It was about some men who rode boats down river rapids. It had looked very exciting. Then and there, Mike had decided that he wanted to try it. Now, the only thing he had to do was find a boat and learn how to use it. But he kept his thoughts to himself.

When Mike got back to his grandfather's cabin, he was tired. His grandfather was not there. He had left a note on the table. The note said that Hank had gone into town for supplies.

Mike ate an apple from the pile on the table. Then he went back outside. He wanted to look around his grandfather's place.

In the back, there was a small garden. There was also a shed. It was full of boards and things. Next to the shed was an old garage. Mike opened the garage. He stopped short. In front of him was a boat. Next to the boat was a space large enough for a car. There was oil on the ground. His grandfather must have some kind of car, he thought. He wondered if Hank would let him drive it. Mike knew how to drive. But he was too young to get a license.

Just then, a beat-up old truck came into the yard. Mike got out of the way. Hank drove the truck into the garage. He got out. He was carrying a bag of food. Canardly jumped out after him.

"Well," said Hank. "I see you have been looking around the place. How do you like it?"

Mike made himself smile. "Great," he said. "You have a great place here, Hank."

"Well, glad you like it," Hank said. He looked down at Canardly. The dog was resting on the ground. "The dog is really glad, too. Right, Canardly?"

Canardly didn't even move. Mike looked at Hank. He wondered why Hank was talking to the dog. The old man was not even smiling.

"Say," said Mike. "I see you have a boat out there in the garage. Do you ever use it?"

Hank gave him a look. "Why, of course I do, boy," he said. "I take her out on the lake every now and then. I catch a nice pile of fish for supper."

"Do you ever take it out on the river?" Mike asked.

Hank made a noise. "Of course not!" he said. "Only a fool would take a boat out on that river. Or somebody who can really handle a boat."

"Oh!" said Mike.

Hank looked at him. "Of course, when I was younger, now," he said, "I *could* really handle a boat then. And maybe I was a bit of a fool, too. I took a boat—a little larger than the one I have now—down the river about 12 times. Then, one time, I had some bad luck. I hit a rock. The whole bottom of the boat pulled off. Broke my leg. And I swallowed a lot of water. I had a bad time getting to a place where somebody could help me. Came near to dying before I was found. That was the last time I rode her."

Hank stood quiet for a minute. Mike watched him. The story had been frightening. But not enough to make Mike give up the idea of riding the river.

"Will you take me out on the lake some time?" he asked. "I want to learn how to handle the boat."

Hank seemed surprised. "Why, I thought you didn't like anything about the life out here," he said. "At least, that's the idea I got from the way you have been acting. But I'm glad to see that you are taking an interest. I'll take you fishing tomorrow."

Mike grinned. "Thanks," he said. "That would be great."

He could hardly wait until the next day. He didn't care about the fishing. But he would be in the boat. And he could learn how to handle it.

Chapter 5

The Fishing Trip

"Wake up! Wake up, boy!"
Mike heard Hank's voice. He opened his eyes. It was still dark. He sat up quickly. "What's wrong?" he asked.

All at once the light was on. Mike could see Hank's face bending over it.

"Nothing is wrong, you young idiot!" said Hank. "I thought you wanted to go fishing!"

Mike rubbed the sleep out of his eyes. "Well, sure," he said. "But what's that got to do with getting up in the middle of the night?"

Hank looked at Mike and shook his head. "It's not the middle of the night, boy," he said. "It's almost 4:30 in the morning. If you're going fishing, you have to get an early start. The fish bite best just after the sun comes up."

Mike tried to hide a yawn. He climbed out of bed. The room was cold. He was still half asleep. Why had he ever said he wanted to go fishing?

They drove away from the cabin, pulling the boat behind them. The sky was just turning light. It was a pretty sight. Also, the air smelled good. Clean and fresh. Mike guessed that there were some good things about living out in the woods.

The lake was as still as blue glass. Mike and Hank were the only people around. They got the boat into the water. They put in the fishing gear. Hank threw in a lunch that he had packed.

"Now, boy," said Hank. "There are things about a boat that you should know. First, and most important, it can tip over if you move too fast. You have to get in carefully. And once you're in, don't jump around."

Mike nodded. But inside, he felt a little angry. Hank was talking to him as if he were a baby. Of course, Mike had never been in a boat before. But it didn't seem like any big thing.

Hank got into the boat first. He picked up the oars. "I'll row first," he said. "But you're going to have to do your part, too. I'll get us out a ways. Then I'll let you take over."

Mike watched Hank row. The old man moved his upper body forward. Then he pulled back on the oars. It didn't look too hard.

"No, no, boy!" Hank said, a few minutes later. "Not like that! You have to get them into the water at the same time!"

Sweat was running down into Mike's eyes. He didn't know if he wanted to yell or cry or both. It had looked so easy. But it was not easy at all.

The oars were much heavier than they had looked when Hank was rowing. Mike could not seem to get them into the water at the same time. The boat was going around in circles in the middle of the lake.

"You have to pull on them evenly, boy! Pull on them evenly!"

Mike started to talk to himself under his breath. He was trying as hard as he could. He thought there was probably something wrong with the boat.

"Here, boy," Hank said at last. "Let's stop for now. This is a good spot. Let's do a little fishing. I just saw a fish jump, over there."

Mike took a deep breath. He pulled the oars up into the oar locks, as Hank had told him. Hank handed him a rod and reel. "You know how to use this, boy?" he asked.

Mike shook his head. Oh great, he thought. Another lesson!

Hank showed him how to use the rod and reel. Mike tried to listen. He didn't want to make a fool of himself again.

Hank helped Mike let his line down into the water. Then Hank threw his own line far out into the lake. He reeled it in a little. Then he sat back.

Just at that moment, Mike felt a pull on his line. All of a sudden he felt very excited. He had a fish on his line! He tried to remember what Hank had told

him. But he could not think of a thing. He only knew
that he had a fish on his line. And he had to bring it
in.

He pulled hard on his pole. He jumped to his feet.
He heard his grandfather yell. And then Mike was
falling.

A second later, the cold water of the lake closed
over his head.

Chapter 6

Learning from Hank and Jo

In a few minutes, Mike came to the top. The shock of the cold water made him open his mouth wide. He swallowed some water.

He could see the bottom of the upturned boat. It was just in front of him. He saw Hank hanging onto the side of the boat. Hank was looking all around. He appeared very worried. Mike could see that his grandfather was afraid for him. But when Hank saw Mike, he started to yell. "You young fool! What are you trying to do? Drown us both?"

Hank took hold of Mike's clothes and pulled him over to the boat. "We are going to have to try to push this boat to shore," Hank said. "I don't suppose you can swim."

"I'm a good swimmer!" Mike said loudly.

"Well, at least that's something," said Hank.

Pushing the boat was hard work. It seemed to Mike as if they were moving only a few inches at a time. His arms were aching.

Then he heard the roar of a motor. He could see a small boat coming toward him. The boat came to a stop just a few feet away. Jo was in the boat. She looked at them. Then she grinned. At that moment, Mike wished he could turn *her* boat over. He wanted to throw *her* into the water.

Still, he had to admit that she didn't rub it in. She could have said something smart. But she didn't. She just helped them into her boat. She took them to shore. Then she and Hank went back and brought in Hank's boat.

When Hank was back on shore, he said, "We can go home now. But we are coming out again. Tomorrow morning!"

He looked at Mike, as if daring him to say something. Mike just nodded. He was getting pretty tired of Hank. The old man acted as though Mike didn't know anything. "I'll show him," Mike said to himself. "And soon, too. I'll learn how to use the boat. And when I'm ready, I'll pack it with food. Then I'll head down the river. *That* will show the old man."

Over the next few weeks, Mike studied hard. He worked more than he ever had in school. He listened

to everything that Hank said. The older man seemed to be pleased by Mike's sudden change. Hank taught Mike how to get along in the woods. He showed him how to fish. And most important, he showed him how to handle the boat.

Mike really tried hard. He found that he learned very quickly. He was also getting used to the kind of

food his grandfather made. He had to admit that he felt stronger. He had more energy. He didn't even miss the junk food he used to eat.

Mike spent a lot of time with Jo. She taught him things, too—like what he could eat if he was lost in the woods.

Mike asked her things about the river. He was afraid to ask Hank too much. Hank might wonder why Mike wanted to know so much. Then he might figure out what Mike meant to do.

"What kind of boats do they use to go down the river?" Mike asked Jo one day.

"My uncle uses rubber boats," she said. "They don't break up on the rocks. Some other kinds do."

"What about wood boats like Hank's?" asked Mike.

Jo nodded her head. "Sometimes they use those," she said. "But Hank's boat is pretty small. Usually they use boats that are specially built. Say, you are really excited about all this, aren't you?"

He nodded. He wondered how much he could tell her. "I want to go down the river some day," he said.

"Maybe you will," she said. "You know, you have changed a lot since you first came here. You have learned a lot, too. If you stay here, maybe in a year or so you will be ready. Maybe I will be ready, too. We can go together."

Mike could not meet her eyes. He didn't dare tell her that he meant to go down the river sooner than that. Much sooner!

Chapter 7

Getting Ready

About a week after Mike's talk with Jo, a letter came from his mother. It said that she was leaving the hospital. She was not well enough to go home yet. They were putting her in a special rest home. It would be two or three months before she was really well.

The letter made Mike feel sad and alone. His mother was with strangers. And so was he. Hank might be his grandfather. But he still acted as though Mike was a stranger.

Mike sat on the front steps. He held the letter in his hand. His grandfather came out of the cabin. He looked at the letter in Mike's hand. Then the old man looked away. He walked right on past Mike. Hank didn't even ask how his own daughter was.

In that moment, Mike made up his mind. Tomorrow would be the day. First, he would get his things together. He would put them in the boat. Then he would go down the river.

Hank came back to tell Mike that he was going into town that afternoon. Mike asked if he could go along. He had a few dollars that his mother had given him. There had been no chance to spend the money out in the woods. Now Mike was glad. There were some things he needed to get for the trip.

They got back to the cabin a few hours later. Mike said he didn't feel well. He said he was going inside to rest.

Hank went outside. He started to work in the garden. While Hank was busy, Mike took the food he thought he would need. He put the food in some plastic he had bought. Then, he coated some match heads with wax from a candle. This was something Hank had told him about. It would keep the matches dry.

Mike put the matches in plastic. Then he lined the picnic basket with plastic. He put the food inside. He knew the basket would float. If the boat turned over, he might be able to save the food. He put the matches into his pocket.

He had taken one of the fishing poles from the garage. He put this in plastic, too. He tied several big pieces of cork to it. That way it would float. The hooks and leaders he put into his pockets. He also put in a big, old jackknife. It belonged to Hank.

Hank had said it would take about two days to make it down to the mouth of the river. But he had also told Mike what could happen if the boat turned over. It could take several days to walk out of the woods. Mike wanted to do this right. He was going to be prepared for everything.

He remembered to take a second pair of shoes. He also took an old blanket he had found. It would be cold at night.

Hank was still out in the garden. Mike took all of the things out to the boat in the garage. He put them under the wide back seat. Then he returned to the cabin. He was ready.

In the early morning, before the sun was even beginning to come up, Mike got out of bed. He put on his clothes. He carried his shoes in his hand.

Hank was asleep in the small room off the kitchen. Mike walked quietly into the room. Hank kept the keys to the truck hanging on a hook on the wall. Mike took them down. The keys made a little noise. But Hank didn't wake up.

Mike put on his shoes. He went to the door. In a few minutes, he was in the garage.

It took him a little while to get the boat and trailer hooked up to the car. He had to let the truck out of gear. Then he had to push it out of the garage. It had to be right in front of the trailer. He was glad that the garage was on a small hill.

Mike finally got the trailer hooked up. Then he let the truck roll down the hill. He went quite a way from the cabin. Then he turned the key and started the truck. It seemed to be making a lot of noise. He looked behind him. No light came on in the cabin. He put the old truck in gear. Then he drove away. He could hardly wait to get to the river.

Chapter 8

Riding the Rapids

Mike backed the truck toward the river. He wanted to put the boat into the water under the bridge. The water was quiet there.

He had a little trouble backing the truck and the trailer up to the water. He had to pull forward and then back up again. He finally got it right. Then he put the boat into the water. He climbed into the boat. With one oar, he pushed away from the bank.

He rowed out into the middle of the river. He could feel the current take the boat. He remembered what

Jo and Hank had said. He knew he would not have to do much more rowing. The current would carry him down the river. All he would have to do is use the oars to keep the boat away from rocks and other things in the water.

In a little while, the sun came up over the trees. Mike took out the food that he had brought along for breakfast. He ate a roll and some meat. The boat was moving faster now. The trees along the bank were taller. Mike saw one or two people fishing from the shore.

Mike began to get tired of sitting. He started to look for a place to land and make camp. He knew he would be coming to the rapids pretty soon. Once he was in the rapids, he would not be able to stop and rest.

He looked in front of him to the left. He saw what looked like a good place to land. It was a wide beach. He started to use the oars to turn toward the shore. But the boat would not go the way he wanted it to. Instead, it went faster. It kept going right down the middle of the river.

Mike was beginning to get frightened now. He began to work hard. He pulled on the right oar. He tried to get the boat out of the current. It was no use. The boat was already going past the little beach.

Mike was really scared now. He could not even get the boat to shore here. How would he get it through the rapids?

The shores and the trees were going by faster and faster. The boat began to rock and shake. Mike could see rocks sticking up out of the water.

Then, in front of him, he could see white water. It was the rapids! Sweat broke out on Mike's face.

Before he had started the trip, he had not really
been worried about getting through the rapids. But
now he could see that he was in real trouble.

He held on tightly to the oars. First he moved the
left one. Then he moved the right. The rocks were
closer together now. There was not much room
between them.

All at once, with a rush, he was into clear water
again. The rapids were gone. Mike let out his
breath. His arms felt heavy. His whole back hurt. It
had been hard. But he had made it through all right.

Mike could see a large cliff around the bend. He
could not see the other side. He rubbed his hands
together. They were tired, and they hurt. The boat

raced on. It went around the cliff. Then Mike saw the rapids. The *real* rapids. They were walled by high cliffs on each side. They went on for as far as he could see. Mike looked at the rushing white water. He had never been more afraid.

Quickly, he pulled his jacket from under the seat. He put it on. Then he took out some of the food. He put it into his pocket. He also put some of it under his jacket. That was all he had time to do. Then the rapids caught the boat.

Mike reached forward. He picked up the oars. He tried to keep the boat away from the rocks. But the rocks were all around. The oars seemed to have a life of their own. Mike was not strong enough to handle them.

The boat rocked from side to side. Mike almost fell out of his seat. The right oar was pulled from his hand. It snapped against a rock. He held the left oar with both hands. But it was pulled away into the water.

Then the boat was pushed sideways. Mike hung onto the sides. He was too scared to do anything else.

Everything was happening so fast. Suddenly Mike was knocked forward. He heard the sound of breaking wood. The next moment, he felt the icy waters of the river pulling at his body.

Chapter 9

Overturned

For a minute, Mike's head was under water. Then he was pushed to the top. A moment later, he was thrown against the rocks.

The wind was knocked out of him. He tried to grab the wet stone. There was no place to get hold of it. He was pulled away again. For a second, he saw the boat. It was broken into two pieces.

Then all he could see was foam. He could not get any air. Spray was all around. He felt himself hit

another rock. This time he didn't hit so hard. And this time he was in luck. He could see that he had been washed up near shore. The water was not so fast there. He was able to get hold of the rock. He could keep himself from being washed away again.

For a while, he just rested. He waited until he felt stronger. He was numb with cold. He knew he had to move while he still could.

He could see another rock closer to shore. Carefully, he moved from his rock to the next rock. Finally, he made it to shore. Then he passed out on the bank.

A few minutes later, Mike opened his eyes. At first he didn't know where he was. But then he sat up and saw the river, and he remembered. By then it was growing quite dark. He was cold all the way through. His side hurt badly.

He pulled himself to his feet. He knew he would have to make a fire. He had to get warmed up. He didn't want to die from the cold.

He thought of the matches in his pocket. With cold fingers, he hunted for them. They were still there. There was not much light. But he was able to find some small sticks. He got the fire started.

He took off his wet jacket and shoes. He spread them out to dry near the fire. Then he took out the food from his jacket. The food was still dry because of the plastic. He thought of Hank. Hank had told him to put on a jacket if he ever thought his boat was going to turn over. Without Hank, he would not have had the matches or the food.

He found a large piece of dead wood. And he put it on the fire. He placed it so that it would burn for a long time. Hank had taught him that, too. Mike lay down by the fire. He put the food next to his body. In a moment, he was asleep.

He woke up soon after the sun came up. The fire had burned out. But his clothes were about half dry. He tried to get up. He found that he could hardly move. He pulled up his clothes and looked down at his side. It was black and blue. It hurt to touch it.

Mike made himself get dressed and walk around. He took out some of the food and ate it. He ate only a little. He didn't know how long it would be before he got out of there.

He put the rest of the food into his jacket. Then he tied the jacket to a tree branch. Hank had told him not to leave his food where animals could get to it. Then Mike went to look in the water. He wanted to see if he could find his fishing gear or the food basket.

He didn't find anything. But he noticed something. Something that made him feel more lost than ever. Just a little way from where he was standing, there was no river bank at all. Nothing but tall cliffs on each side of the river. Hank had told him that if he ever became lost, he should follow a river. He had said that there were usually houses or people along a river. But now there was no way Mike could do that. He would have to head into the woods.

Mike went back to his camp. He sat down by the dead fire to think. It seemed to him that there were two things he could do. He could head into the forest. Or he could stay where he was. If he went into the forest, he would have no idea which way to go. Also, he had no way to carry water with him. If he stayed where he was, his food could give out. But he would have water to drink. Maybe he could even catch a fish or two.

He remembered the first day he had come to stay with his grandfather. He had been lost. He had decided to stay in one place. Well, his grandfather had laughed at him. But Hank *had* said that staying in one place was usually the best thing to do when you were lost. Mike made up his mind to stay where he was.

Just deciding made him feel a little better. He started to work at making his camp. He put a ring of stones around the dead fire. Then he heard the sound of a motor.

At first it was hard to hear over the roaring of the river. But pretty soon he knew there was no mistake. He could see a helicopter flying toward him.

Chapter 10

Starting Over

Mike blocked out the sun with his hand. He looked up. The helicopter was moving slowly. It looked as if the people inside were looking for something.

Mike knew that it would be hard for them to see him. He ran to the edge of the river. He took off his jacket. He waved it over his head. He jumped up and down and yelled. He didn't even notice how much his side hurt.

Soon the helicopter was right over him. The pilot looked out and waved. Then a voice came over a bullhorn. "Are you all right?"

Mike nodded and waved.

"We can't land here," the pilot said. "We have to let down a rope ladder. Can you climb it?"

Mike didn't even think of his hurt side. He nodded yes.

The helicopter hovered. The pilot let down a long swinging ladder. The ladder kept blowing around in the wind. Finally, Mike got hold of the bottom rung. He climbed a few rungs. Then he rested for a moment. It was not easy. He paid no attention to the pain in his side. He climbed up.

In just a few minutes, strong arms pulled him inside the helicopter. He looked up and saw his grandfather's face. Then his side started to hurt so badly that he passed out.

When Mike woke up, he was in a white bed in a light green room. The next thing he saw was Hank's face. The old man was bending over the bed.

"You all right, boy?" Hank asked in a low voice.

Mike nodded. He tried to move. He found that his body was tightly wrapped. He looked up at Hank.

"You cracked a few ribs, son," Hank said. "And you have a lot of black and blue spots all over you. But it's nothing too bad. You are going to be fine."

Mike swallowed. He thought of the broken boat and the other things that were lost. He also thought about all the worry that he had put Hank through. Then he thought about his mother.

"I'm sorry, Hank!" he said. "I know I was wrong. I was wrong to take your boat. I was wrong to think I knew enough to ride that river. The only thing that kept me from dying was that I remembered everything you and Jo told me. I'm really sorry. Does my mother know?"

Hank nodded. Mike felt terrible. His mother was really sick. And he had done something that would worry her. It might make her sicker. How had she felt when she heard that he had disappeared?

Hank smiled suddenly. "I didn't tell her anything until *after* we found you," he said. "No use worrying her until we knew for sure what had happened."

Mike felt tears come to his eyes. He reached over and took his grandfather's hand. "Thanks," Mike said.

Hank held Mike's hand. "Think nothing of it, boy," he said. "I always figure that family should stick together."

Mike looked up at him in surprise.

Hank's face was red. "This is what I'm trying to say, boy," he said. "While you were out there on that river, I did some thinking. I didn't know if I would ever see you again. And I knew that I would miss you, that I cared about you. Yes, and I still care about your mother, too."

Mike was too surprised to say anything.

His grandfather went on. "Now, I want to make a plan with you. You and I, well, we can start all over again. And when your ma is well enough, she can come out here to us. We can make the cabin into a real home. What do you say?"

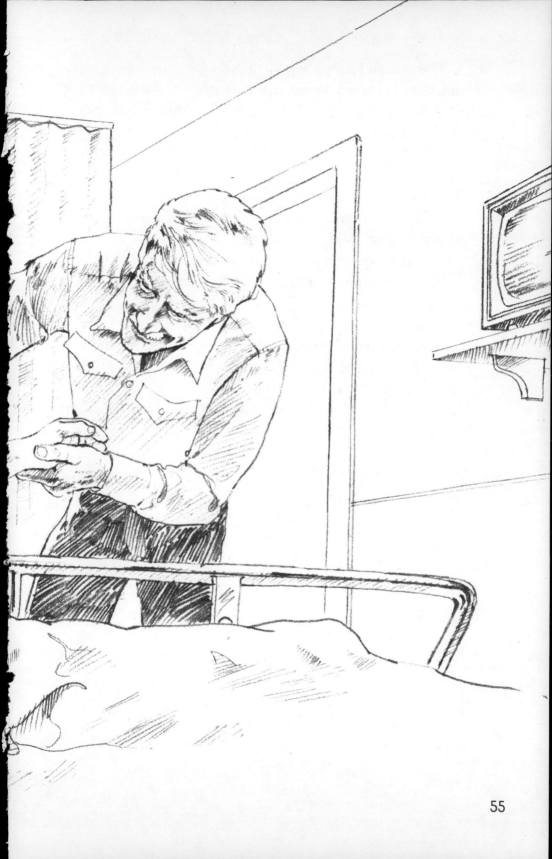

Mike didn't know what to say. He only knew what he felt. He tried to sit up and put his arms around Hank. Hank reached over and hugged him back. The old man was careful of the cracked ribs.

"Well," said Hank. "You have another visitor waiting. Jo came with me. Then I had better get home to Canardly. He was pretty excited when I told him that you were all right. I'm afraid he might tear the place up while I'm gone!"

"Thank you, Hank," Mike whispered.

Hank smiled and got up. He walked toward the door. Then he turned around.

"And by the way," he said, "from now on you better call me Grandpa. I'm not sure I like this new idea of kids calling old people by their first names. It's just not dignified!"

Hank walked out the door. Mike smiled as he watched him go. He had never felt happier.